STABLE GIRL

STABLE GIRL

WORKING FOR THE FAMILY

written by Patricia Harrison Easton

photographed by Herb Ferguson

Harcourt Brace Jovanovich, Publishers

SAN DIEGO NEW YORK LONDON

HBJ

Library of Congress Cataloging-in-Publication Data
Easton, Patricia Harrison.
Stable girl/written by Patricia Harrison Easton:
photographed by Herb Ferguson. — 1st ed.
p.   cm.
Summary: Portrays a day in the life of Danielle,
who works in her family's racing stable and helps
in the family business of training racehorses.
ISBN 0-15-278340-7
1. Harness racing — Juvenile literature.
2. Stables — Management — Juvenile literature.
3. Standardbred horse — Juvenile literature.
4. Snyder, Danielle — Juvenile literature.
[1. Harness racing. 2. Stables — Management.
3. Standardbred horse.
4. Horses. 5. Snyder, Danielle.]
I. Ferguson, Herb, ill. II. Title.
SF339.E18   1991
798.4'6'092 — dc20   90-45619

First edition
A B C D E

The photographs for this book were taken with a Nikon F-3 with
motor drives and a Nikon 8000 using Kodachrome 64 and 200 film.
Composition by Thompson Type, San Diego, California
Color separations by Bright Arts, Ltd., Singapore
Printed and bound by Tien Wah Press, Singapore
Production supervision by Warren Wallerstein and Ginger Boyer
Designed by Kathleen Westray

To Danielle and her family,
especially to the memory of her grandpa Dick Snyder.
— P. E.

To my wife, Ann,
who has put up with my addiction for taking photographs
of everything and anything no matter where we are
or at what time of day it might be.
— H. F.

ACKNOWLEDGMENTS

We wish to thank Ladbroke at The Meadows
for their enthusiastic support of this project.

I am working today. There's a lot of work to do around a racing stable. Ours is the Snyder Stable, and we train and race thirty horses at The Meadows racetrack. A lot of stables are smaller than ours, but none here is bigger.

Our whole family helps in the business. My dad, Dane Snyder, trains the horses. My uncle Doug drives the horses when they race. My mom does all the paperwork and sends out the bills. My sister, Alecia, has two horses to groom this summer.

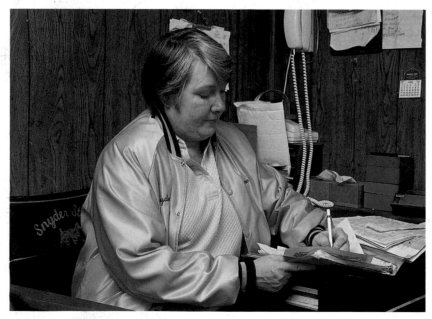

And I'm Danielle. I help wherever I'm needed. Today I'm needed at the barn.

Work starts early at the racetrack. Ab, our second trainer, is at the barn by six o'clock to feed the horses. The grooms arrive around seven. We drive through the guard gate by seven-thirty.

Before I start to work, I run to see my favorite horse, Actron. I think I'm his favorite person, because he whinnies when he hears my voice. Actron sticks his big head over his stall guard for his morning kiss. He sniffs my pockets for the carrot I always bring him. Today I give him an extra carrot because he's in a race tonight. I tell him it's his good luck carrot.

Actron doesn't belong to us. Some of the horses are ours, but most are owned by people who pay Dad and Uncle Doug to train and race them. It doesn't matter who owns them — every horse in our stable gets the same good care.

Our horses are standardbred racehorses. They are a different breed from the thoroughbred racehorses that run in races like the Kentucky Derby.

One difference between our horses and thoroughbreds is that our horses don't gallop when they race. They either trot or pace. A trot is just like the trot of any horse — the left front foot moves forward at the same time as the right hind foot — but a lot faster. When they pace, the left front foot and left hind foot move forward together. Breeding determines which gait a horse will prefer.

Our kind of racing is called harness racing because the horses wear a harness and pull a racing bike called a sulky.

"Good morning, Danielle," Ab calls. He's in the stall with Roselyn S., our three-year-old pacer. Rosie was named after my grandma. Like Grandma, she's pretty and gentle.

Ab leads Rosie into the aisle to harness her. He slides the crupper under Rosie's tail and pulls the girth up behind her shoulders. He tightens the girth to make sure it's snug. Then he slips the bridle over her head. I help by attaching the lines to the bit. Next Ab hitches her to the cart and off they go to the track for Rosie's morning workout.

Dad and Uncle Doug check the schedule for the day. "Actron has an appointment with the blacksmith to get new shoes," Dad says.

"I'll take him, Dad," I offer and run to get a lead shank.

Actron prances and tosses his head as I lead him to the blacksmith shop. "Settle down, now," I say, and he listens to me. We don't have far to go. Larry Caldwell is our blacksmith, and his shop is right behind our barn.

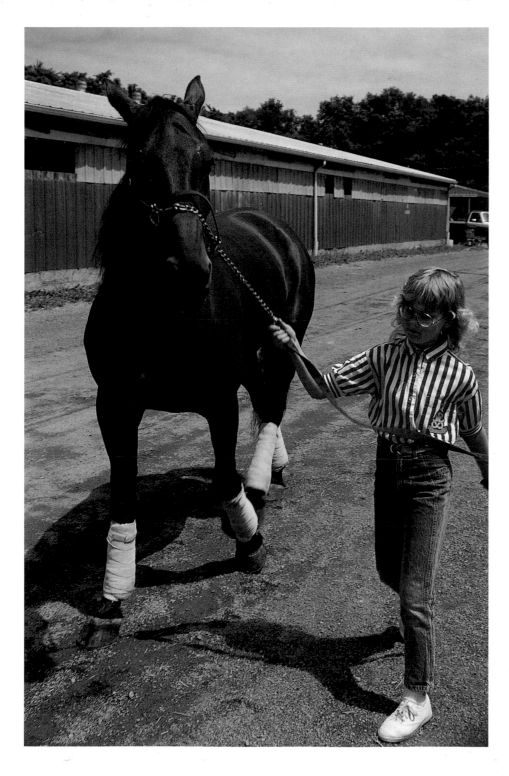

Fifteen blacksmiths rent shops on the grounds. My teacher at school says they should be called farriers, but to everyone around here they are "blacksmiths."

Larry is waiting for us. He takes Actron's lead shank and fastens him into the crossties.

"When can I come back for him?" I ask.

"Give me about an hour, Danielle," he says.

When I return to the barn, Uncle Doug and Dad each have a colt harnessed and ready to go. Today is a training day for them.

Most days our horses only jog conditioning miles. When a horse is scheduled to jog, his groom drives him at an easy gait clockwise around the outside rail of the track. Training miles are driven by trainers — Dad, Uncle Doug, or Ab — instead of grooms. A training mile is almost like a real race. The horses go fast counter-clockwise around the track — the same direction as when they race. Someday I'll be able to train just like Dad and Uncle Doug.

Alecia comes around the corner. "Hey, Danielle," she says. "I'll make you a deal— fifty cents each to muck out my stalls for me."

"Make it a dollar and you've got a deal." I know how much Alecia hates to clean stalls. I also know how much Dad pays her. She can afford the two dollars.

Alecia agrees.

Pushing the wheelbarrow to the first stall, I get to work. Don't get me wrong: It's not that I love to clean stalls—I just don't hate it as much as Alecia does. I stab the pitchfork under a fresh pile of manure and lift it into the wheelbarrow. Next I sift through the straw to make sure I don't miss any wet spots underneath. When the stall is clean, I toss an extra flake of straw around. Both stalls are finished before Dad and Uncle Doug come back with the colts.

As I walk by the washroom, I hear the dryer shut off. Inside, I find a big load of clean leg bandages. These strips of elastic are pretty important around here. If a horse has sore legs, bandaging them provides extra support and helps to keep them sound. Some horses jump around in their stalls or kick the walls. We bandage their legs so they don't hurt them.

Rolling leg bandages was my first job at the barn when I was too little to help with the horses. Now it's something I do while I'm resting between jobs.

The end of a bandage dances along the ground as I pull it toward me. Our cat, Tyke, bats at it with her front paws until the bandage starts to climb up my leg. Then she leaps up beside me, purring.

"Why don't you wrap a set of those bandages around Rosie's legs," calls Ab.

Inside her stall, I fasten Rosie in the crossties. She lowers her head and blows puffs of air down my neck, giving me goosebumps. I rub her nose. "I can't play now, Rosie. I have to get my work done," I tell her. When I finish, I stand back and check her legs. Good — a nice, neat job — snug, but not too tight.

"The Snyder Stable, call the switchboard," announces the loudspeaker outside of our barn.

I'm the only Snyder not too busy to answer the page. In the office I phone the switchboard. "This is Danielle Snyder," I say. "Do you have a message for us?"

The program office needs the eligibility papers on one of our new horses. These papers show the horse's complete racing record. The program office keeps records for all the horses on the track. That way they make sure all the horses in a race can go about the same speed.

I climb the hill to the administration building and run upstairs to the offices. As I hand the papers to Curby, the program director, I see the clock on her desk. "Oh, my gosh," I yell. "I've got to pick up Actron at the blacksmith shop." I'm almost through the door when I hear Curby laugh.

"This is the first time a Snyder has left my office without raiding my candy jar," she says.

"I don't want to spoil our record," I say as I reach for the butterscotch candies. "Thanks, but I have to go."

I pop one of the candies into my mouth and shove the rest into my pocket for later.

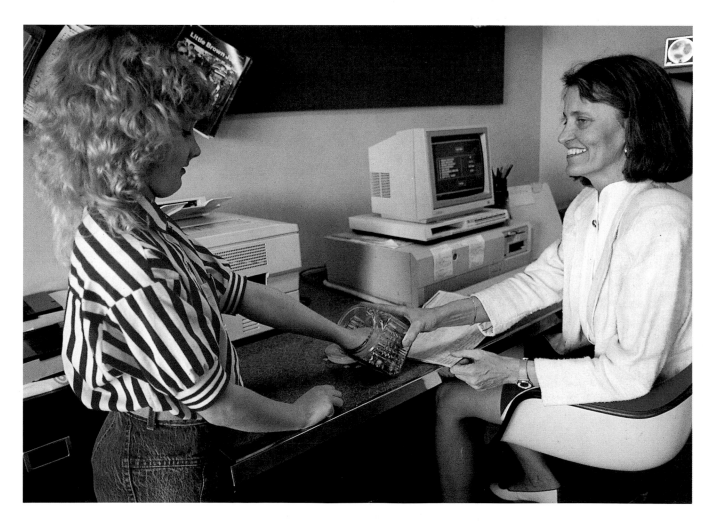

When I get to the blacksmith shop, Larry is taking Actron's last shoe from the fire to shape it on the anvil. Like most blacksmiths, Larry orders horseshoes ready-made. They come in all sizes and shapes. He uses his small propane forge to heat the metal shoes until they soften enough for him to shape them.

Larry hammers and shapes the shoe, then holds it to Actron's hoof to check the fit. He rubs away some of the hoof with a file so the shoe will fit better. None of this hurts Actron, any more than cutting my fingernails hurts me. The outer covering of a horse's hoof has no feeling.

While Larry nails the shoe in place, I pick up some of the hoof trimmings from the floor and shove them into my pocket. Larry smiles. He knows I take them home to our dog — they're just like candy to her.

Back at our barn I see the veterinarian's truck parked outside. He's here to see our colt Obie Hanover. Obie hasn't been racing well, and Dad thinks something may be wrong with him.

I hurry to put Actron back into his stall. Dad calls for me to bring him the twitch. I arrive with it as Dr. Parry and his assistant walk into the barn carrying a big bottle of medicine and some tubing.

Dad pulls Obie's upper lip through the twitch and twists the chain snugly around it. The twitch doesn't cut the lip or really hurt Obie, but the pressure keeps his attention on his lip instead of on what Dr. Parry is doing to him. Horses are a lot stronger than we are. If we didn't have a few ways to outsmart them, we'd never be able to take care of them, especially when they're hurt.

Dr. Parry gives Obie an intravenous solution of vitamins with electrolytes, and then, because he thinks Obie may be sore in one of his hocks, he injects the joint with some medicine.

Before he leaves, Dr. Parry promises to check on Obie again in a few days.

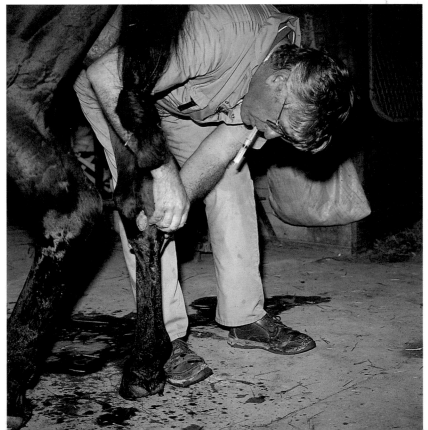

I walk over to the schedule board. Our trotter Harry Robinson is supposed to swim this morning. The Meadows has a spa with a swimming pool and whirlpools for the horses. Harry has been a little footsore lately, so swimming is better for him than pounding around the track.

George comes out of Obie's stall. I catch his eye and point to Harry's name on the schedule.

George knows what I want and winks at me. "Well," he says, "I had better get Harry to the spa." He calls to my dad: "You know, Dane, I could use Danielle's help in case old Harry decides to drown himself."

Dad laughs. "All right. Get going."

When we reach the pool, Harry whinnies. Harry's not too sure about swimming. The first time we tried to swim him he leaped from the top of the ramp, fell on his knees, and slid headfirst into the pool. The water is eleven feet deep, and George had a hard time pulling Harry back to the surface. That's why they all joke about Harry trying to drown himself.

George attaches a long pole to Harry's halter and walks him to the ramp. Today Harry walks down the ramp into the water without any trouble. When he's belly-deep, he starts to float. Then he begins to swim, pumping his legs as if he were trotting on the track. George walks beside him on the rim of the pool. With the long pole, George can push Harry back if he tries to climb out.

"Here, Danielle. You take over," George says. "This big fella isn't going to climb out on us." I take the pole and walk around the outside of the pool as Harry does his laps.

When our time is up, George takes the pole from me. George guides Harry to the ramp and out he comes. At the top of the ramp Harry shakes, spraying water all over us.

I run a metal scraper over Harry's neck and sides, squeezing more water from his coat. George runs the scraper over his back where I can't reach. Even though it's a warm day, we throw a lightweight blanket on him to keep him from getting a chill on the way to the barn. If Harry gets chilled he could get stiff muscles.

On the way back George tells me about the kittens he found in the straw this morning. We walk by the Altmeyer barn. My friends Heather and Julie Altmeyer have come to work with their dad. I see Julie sweeping the barn aisle and Heather cleaning harness.

"Come and see our kittens when you're done," I call. Their dad says they can come now, so we leave George to lead Harry back and run ahead to our barn.

Mom shows us the kittens. They are tumbled over each other, sleeping in the straw. Mom says they look to be about a month old. Their mother must have been hiding them. Heather, Julie, and I each pick up a kitten to take outside to play. Mine meows when I rub her against my cheek. She's so soft. "May I take her home, Mom?"

Mom just rolls her eyes and shakes her head. I ask her this every time one of the barn cats has a litter. Someday I may catch her off guard.

"Danielle!" Dad hollers. "How would you like to train Trusty with me?" He and Uncle Doug are heading for the track.

I say good-bye to Julie and Heather. We agree to meet at the races tonight. As they leave, I run to Dad and Trusty.

Dad helps me onto the cart seat and then jumps up behind me. When we reach the track, Dad turns Trusty to jog along the outside rail for his warm-up trips and I take the lines. Now I'm the driver.

When Uncle Doug turns his colt and heads for the inside rail, we follow. Dad slips his hands beside mine. As we come to the starting line, Trusty leans into the bit. He quickens his pace. Dad tightens his hold on the lines and so do I. It's time to train!

I can feel the rhythm of Trusty's gait in my arms and shoulders. The wind blows in my face and through my hair. The sharp crack of Trusty's shoes on the ground-limestone surface of the track beats in my ears.

We charge into the paddock turn with Uncle Doug setting the pace. At the top of the stretch Dad pulls Trusty to the outside and we race up beside Uncle Doug. Trusty's legs begin to pump harder, faster. "Come on, Trusty!" I yell. Neck and neck we fly across the finish line, just like in a real race.

Mom has been at the rail watching us. "I see we've got another driver in the family," she calls, and I nod, trying to catch my breath.

Before I leave for the day, I walk Actron around the barn, letting him nibble at the grass along the drive. Since he's racing tonight, he won't get jogged or have a workout today. Walking him will help keep his muscles loose.

"Danielle, it's one o'clock. Dad's ready to go home," calls Alecia.

I lead Actron back to his stall and give him a kiss on his warm, velvety nose. "Good luck tonight," I whisper before running to the car.

That night I meet Heather and Julie at the Two Minute Club. Owners and horsemen and their families crowd the tables. Mom sits with her friends at the top level of the dining room. Julie and Heather and I have our own table in the front by the window. The waitress brings us soft drinks and extra baskets of popcorn.

Outside, everyone hustles about his work. The drivers are dressed in their registered colors as they take their warm-up turns around the track. Back in the paddock, the grooms hurry, carrying water to the horses and adjusting harness straps. The horses toss their heads and paw the dirt in front of their stalls. Like all of us, they sense the excitement. Race night is what all their training and all our hard work are about.

When the races start, we go outside and stand along the rail, cheering for our horses. When our stable doesn't have a horse in a race, I help Julie and Heather cheer for their horse. Sometimes we meet other friends in front of the Club. That way we have a horse to cheer for in every race.

Actron is in the fifth race. He tosses his head as he paces in front of the grandstand. My mom says if we take good care of our horses, it will show on race night. Actron's coat shines as he prances past us.

The horses fall into place behind the gate, and off they go toward the starting line. I hold my breath as the wings of the gate swing shut. A moment later the announcer shouts, "They're off!"

Actron is pacing in third place along the rail. That's a good position for now. The front horses are going pretty fast, but by holding Actron in place Uncle Doug will save him for the finish.

At the half, one of the horses behind Actron makes his move, pulling around two horses and pacing fast. Uncle Doug hears him coming and pulls Actron from the rail. That's what Actron was waiting for! He passes the second horse, and by the three-quarter pole he's gaining on the horse in the lead.

"Come on, Actron!" I yell. I jump up and down, yelling louder. Julie and Heather join in. Down the stretch the horses come. Actron passes the hip, the flank, the shoulder of the lead horse. The two horses are nose to nose as they pass in front of us. Then Actron takes the lead and paces across the finish line, the winner by a length.

My whole family goes to the winner's circle to get our picture taken. Everyone is smiling for the photographer. It feels good knowing we all helped Actron get here.